Esmarelda's Shoe

PAGE PUBLISHING
Conneaut Lake, PA

First originally published by Page Publishing 2022

ISBN 978-1-6624-7637-2 (pbk)
ISBN 978-1-6624-7638-9 (digital)

Printed in the United States of America

Esmarelda's Shoe

Edee Troncale

On Halloween night, everyone is ready for a fright, but this is the night that Esmarelda will take flight.

3

You see, when you are walking down the street from house to house, there is a witch that makes sure everything is just right. She swoops through the night, making sure all children are kept in her sight.

You feel something as if it is a hummingbird flying around, but it is Esmarelda not making a sound.

She can be small, or she can stand tall. She will drop off one shoe at your house, and she cannot be seen because she is as small as a mouse.

This shoe will sit there waiting on her to return.

11

For she feels for some children, there is a lesson to be learned.

13

If children are good and listen to their parents, then Halloween night will be filled with homes full of candy!

We all know that is just dandy!

On Halloween night, she flies through each house and picks up shoes and doesn't even leave you a clue.

Each shoe is either a right or a left, and no one knows which is which because this is a secret that she has kept.

So tuck yourself in each night, and before you sleep, make sure Esmarelda's shoe is there in sight so all will be good on Halloween night!

Make sure you listen to your parents and teachers because, if not, she might leave you some leeches.

So Happy Halloween from Esmarelda and take care of that shoe because she is watching you too…

If you would like Esmarelda to drop off a shoe at your house—just email her at Esmareldashoe@gmail.com

About the Author

Edee Troncale lives in Panama City Beach, Florida, with her family. She loves telling stories to her grandchildren. Her favorite time of the day is when her grandchildren come over and they play with crafts. Edee loves to be outdoors snuggled in a chair reading a good book. Her family keeps her quite busy with their activities. She loves to draw and create. Her grandchildren were her inspiration for her short story. To her, reading a book allows you to go places that you would never dream that you could go.

CPSIA information can be obtained
at www.ICGtesting.com
Printed in the USA
BVHW021820280922
648123BV00001B/1